A Peek at True Colors

A Peek at True Colors

by
Euphoria

To order additional copies of this book, contact:
Xlibris Corporation
1-888-795-4274
www.Xlibris.com
Orders@Xlibris.com
91820

Acknowledgement

Importantly, I'd like to thank God for blessing me with the knowledge and ability to write this story. I'd also like to express my appreciation to my family and friends for supporting me in my work. Last, but not least, I want to consider the printing staff for all their hard work and services in helping me compose this book.

Note to Reader:

Aside from the obvious references to my personal beliefs, the elements of this story is purely fictional. Any resemblance to people, places, or circumstances is purely conincidental.

On a cold windy night, Keva Murlette's lifeless body was discovered, slain. Sustaining a wound to the head, she laid scattered on the floor. Blood slowly profused onto the plush white carpet. Her stringy, damp hair partially hid her rigid face. The lips that were once full of life were pale and speechless. Her sodden, wide eyes stared into the entryway of her bedroom. That joyful, naïve, innocent spirit had abandoned her, leaving her body to perish. A bracelet decorated with ornaments of her life's experiences dangled from her wrist. Chips of paint and blood underneath her nails proved she put up a struggle. The room was silent. Only the sound of the clattering rain against the window pane could be heard. A cool draft brushed the pages of her open book. The window had been left open. The window latch had been broken and clunks of muddy trails coated the window pane. The broken lamp behind her partially lit the room. Blithe detectives soon surrounded her, leaving muddy tracks to follow them. Rubber gloves covered with flims of dust powder tampered with her belongings. From every angle, flashing cameras took advantage of her twisted position. Flickering lights diffused the room, prying her most private possessions. The bedroom that was once a child's dominion had tragically become a murder scene.

Officer Dolopis reached for the door knob. In great pain, he pulled himself up. He looked around then at his watch. He wondered how long he had been lying there. Stammering, he exited the room. He could see tiny claws in the entryway of the door. Crooked family portraits hung in the hallway. He entered the living area to get past trafficing detectives. In transition, he bypassed the child's shocked sibling. He could see an officer consoling her with comforting words. On his way out, Officer Dolopis observed the child's father at the dining table. He calmly cooperated as an officer questioned him. From behind, the coroners slowly carried the body down on a stretcher. Finally reaching the front porch, Officer Dolopis stepped out onto the lawn. Cold drops of rain hit his face. It was still raining. He pulled his drenched hair from his face to gather his senses. Barking bloodhounds ran past him into the night . Broken tree stems and splashes of muddy puddles could be heard as State troopers trailed behind them. They carefully guided their steps with flashlights in search of the suspect. Officers questioned distant neighbors but no one heard nor saw anything. The houses were too far apart for any possible witnesses. It was common for houses on the country side to be set far apart.

Like vultures, Burnbush, Mississippi news reporters ambushed him to get a story. Somehow, he pushed past the mob in an attempt to escape the crime scene. He managed to get through the gate. Downhearted, he stood there with his head held down. From a distance, he could hear a loud screeching noise. The only thing he could see were bright headlights swerving around a curb. Suddenly, the car pulled up in front of the house. Officer Dolopis put his hand up to block the blinding lights. He peeped his head around to get a better view. Only a dim side view could be seen but he knew it was a woman. She threw the car in park, grabbed a sack and leaped out of the car. Unsure of what to expect, she slowed her pace. She gripped the bag for comfort. The walk to the gate seemed distant.

There were police officers everywhere. In circular motion, flashing lights closed in. Yellow tape surrounded the house. By now, she was scared the sound of the sirens rattled her eardrums. Unknowingly, she dropped the groceries and covered her ears. Now taking desperate strides, she searched for her girls. Before she could get to the front gate, an officer blocked her path. Officer Dolopis stood back as he watched her attempt to get past. "This is my house! Let me through!" she cried. By then an officer approached her from behind to restrain her. Still holding her back, the officer said nothing. The sad expression on his face revealed all.

"What's going on? Why won't you let me through?" she pressed. "I'm sorry Mam, but I can't let you in." he finally answered in a trembling voice.

"But I live here! This is my house!" she yelled, struggling to get a lose from the other officer. Suddenly, she was calm. She spotted Officer Dolopis standing nearby. He stood there with his back turned to her. Pacing the dirt ground, he held his head down with both hands in his pockets. He was still out of touch with all that had happened. Unexpectedly, desperate hands grabbed hold of him from behind. He looked down and saw a pair of tiny hands pulling at him. Although tiny, her grip was tight.

"Is my babies alright?" a quivering voice asked. Officer Dolopis slowly turned around to face her. It was the child's mother. She had broken free of the officer's grip. "Did you save my babies?" she cried, grabbing him by the collar now. Officer Dolopis said nothing. His eyes were bloodshot red. He gently broke from her grip and slowly began backing away. "I asked you a question! Did you save my babies?!" she followed.

Almost bumping into something, Officer Dolopis looked down. The driver side door had been left open. He could tell that she had been out grocery shopping. Busted eggs, milk and flower were scattered onto the cracked pavement. She grabbed hold of him again. "I asked you a question, Officer!" she cried, snatching him to and fro.

Hesitant to speak, he finally answered, "Mam, I'm sorry but your daughter was murdered."

"I found her in her bedroom. She had a wound to the head." he explained.

She grabbed her chest as his words cut into her flesh. It felt as if someone had driven a stake through her heart.

"I'm sorry to bring you this news. I promise we'll find the person who did this." he softly said. Slowly, she walked off with a blank look on her face. Officer Dolopis was still talking but she tuned him out. She didn't want to hear anymore.

"No, not my baby! It's not time for her to leave. I'm supposed to go first." she wailed. Her heart dropped to the pit of her stomach. She was devastated. Suddenly, she felt light headed. She looked down. The ground was trembling. Losing her balance, she reached for the gate. Her legs felt weak. She flopped to the damp ground.

Her entire world had been shattered. Crying hysterically, she buried her face in the palm of her hands. She no longer had the desire to live. Holding her head up, she gave a blank stare. She covered her mouth with her trembling hands. In disbelief, she shook her head "No! No! It's not true! This can't be happening!" she wept. Anger consumed her. Quickly, she regained her strength. A sense of destruction came over her. She wanted to rip something apart like her heart had been ripped apart. She jumped to her feet. Who did this?!" she asked in frantic tears.

You let me in to see my babies!" she struggled. "Let.......me....in!" she strained, pushing an officer to get past. Officers attempted to stop her but it was too late. She had already entered into the gate. Her husband slowly approached her. Pulling away from one officer, she met him halfway.

She could see the fear in his eyes as he got closer. "Where's my babies?" she cried. He remained silent. He grabbed her in his arms to console her. Weak from all the pain, she finally gave in, collapsing into his arms.

"What happened? I just went to the store." she wept. Escorting her out of the gate, he guided her back to the car to take a seat.

He purposely blocked her view. He didn't want her to see the coroners.

"Mommy!" her daughter called out. It was Drucilla, her youngest. She ran into her arms. She kneeled down to give her a hug. She squeezed her tight. Her heart rejoiced. Closing her eyes, she buried her face into her hair. She smiled at the scent of her hair. The smell of the strawberry blossom shampoo still lingered in her hair. She never wanted to let her go. One of the medics had been caring for her in the back of the ambulance truck. Kissing her head, she opened her eyes. In search of her other child, she darted her head around Drucilla. Again, her husband attempted to block her view. It was too late. She had already noticed the coroners pushing a trolley bed covered in white sheets onto the porch. "Daddy!" Drucilla called out, reaching for him. He slowly picked her up, gently rubbing her back. Crying, she hugged him tight. Leaving their side, her mother slowly eased around her husband. "Baby wait!" he called out, reaching his arm out to stop her. She walked around to the other side of the gate to get a closer look. The coroners lifted the trolley in an attempt to load it onto the rear of their vehicle. Suddenly, an arm slid from underneath the sheets. The bracelet that she recalled purchasing dangled from the tiny wrist. Right away, she knew it was Keva. She was so overwhelmed with the reunion of her family. So caught up in the moment. Awaiting her child's arrival, she had forgotten what Officer Dolopis had told her. Which one of her daughters were murdered? Which one survived? Those questions never came to her mind. Grabbing hold of the pointed gate, she cried, "No!"

Struggling, she managed to get past the officer inside the gate but that was as far as her strength allowed her. The medics had grabbed her, stopping her in her tracks. "No! I want to see my baby!" she cried, attempting to get past them. She could still see the coroners lifting the trolley onto the rear of the truck but the wheel was stuck. She became desperate. She was insane. "No! Please don't take my baby! Please!" she cried.

Officer Dolopis wanted to do something but there was nothing he could do. He couldn't do anything but watch. He was helpless. He couldn't take it anymore. He just wanted to get away from it all.

Exhaling with discouragement, Officer Dolopis walked past the hysterical mother as medics attempted to sedate her. They wrestled her to the ground to sustain her. Still concerned, he turned around then stopped. He darted his head around them to see if she was alright. Still reaching, she cried, "No! Let me go! You let me see my baby!" from underneath them. He could no longer see her. Her arms were the only thing visible. Only the sound of her intense mourning for her child could be heard. Feeling light headed, she passed out. Unable to bear her suffering, Officer Dolopis dropped to his knees. Sobbing, he covered his face. Suddenly a throbbing pain pierced through his side. He grabbed it to restrain the pain. He groaned as his pain grew intense. He looked at his hands. They were covered in blood. He looked down at his side. His shirt was drenched in blood. He had been hit in his attempt to save the girl. Suddenly, he felt weak. He stumbled onto the last step. He grabbed hold of the rail of the gate for support. Feeling faint, he collapsed. His fellow colleagues suddenly grabbed hold of him. "Officer Dolopis are you alright? An officer has been shot! Officer down! Officer down! Get more medics over here now!" he demanded. Officer Dolopis looked up. It was his partner. Gasping for air, he gripped his side. He laid there as medics surrounded him. He could hardly keep his eyes open. He couldn't hold on any longer. His pupils rolled to the back of his head. He passed out. He could feel rubber hands grabbing hold of him as they lifted him onto a trolley bed. They rolled him onto the back of the ambulance. The medic pulled the oxygen mask over his nose and mouth. Officer Dolopis got a glimpse at his name tag. His name was Steve. Knowing his name gave him some sort of comfort. Maybe because his partner's name was Steve too. He ripped his shirt open. He placed a ceddarroth gauze to the wound then applied pressure. Officer Dolopis frowned at the pain as the medic pierced his skin to give him an IV. His eyes were getting heavier. He dosed off again.

After driving four miles, the truck stopped. Officer Dolopis wanted to open his eyes but couldn't. He could still hear the voices around him.

"What's the problem? Why did we stop?" Steve asked.

"They got the entire street blocked off. There's a horrific fire just blocks up ahead. They say it's a huge apartment complex on fire." the driver answered.

Looking out the window, he asked, "Can't you drive around all this traffic?

"There's no way to get around it." the driver responded.

Officer Dolopis started coughing.

"What are we going to do? This guy's losing a lot of blood."

"Just keep him awake." the driver warned.

"Sir wake up. Stay with me. Just stay with me." he whispered in his ear.

"What's his vital signs?"

"He still has a pulse. And his eyes are still dilated." he answered.

Officer Dolopis could hear the sirens getting louder. They were getting closer.

The driver managed to get a few blocks ahead.

The thick black smoke poured into the streets. The driver could hardly see. The closer he got, the thicker the smoke. Officer Dolopis could feel the starching heat waves coming from the smoke. Sleepily, he opened his eyes, for a moment. He glanced at the double glass window in the back. From a distance, he could see the fire jumping uncontrollably from building to building. The fire was so intense; Firefighters struggled to take control of the flame.

Vaguely, he could see the paramedics lifting patients onto trucks. He closed his eyes again.

The driver turned the radio on to get a news report.

"Turn it up. I can't hear it." Steve yelled from behind.

The driver turned the radio up. "Just this afternoon a firefighter ran into a burning apartment. The firefighter managed to save a child but not himself." Officer Dolopis tilted his head in response to the announcement. A tear rolled down his cheek.

"How's the patient?" the driver asked.

"Still alert." he smiled, signalling him a thumbs up. "How much longer?"

"Only a mile." the driver answered.

Officer Dolopis' eyeballs rolled from side to side as the news reporter spoke. "A doctor in South Carolina committed suicide at 12:00 pm. Doctor Melvin Larke Winthrop of Davenport Memorial Hospital would have been 52 this week. His friends and family said he appeared to be alright but his neighbors claim that he was in debt. They say he kept getting eviction notices on his door to vacate and he couldn't handle it. He leaves behind his wife of 55 years, two sons, one daughter and six grandchildren. He will be greatly missed. And just two days ago a tragedy took place at the Fort Worth Zoo. An animal trainer was attacked and killed by a bear that escaped. If you see this bear please contact animal control at 1-800-ANIMALS. It's sad to say but we just lost a well known mortician, Marcus Beans, at the Heavens Gate Morgue located in Los Angeles, California. He passed at age 31 due to cancer. He worked for that morgue for 15 years. This year would have been his anniversary. He will be greatly missed. If you would like to attend his services you can call 1-800-HEAVENS. In Guam there was a bad tornado storm. Forty people were killed, leaving only 15 people to survive. Its amazing to see how well the community is pulling together to rebuild their homes. Thomas L. Clark was also killed. He was the weather Meterologist for channel 11. He worked for the news station for 32 years. His survivors are his wife of eight years and two children. We are all going to miss him. We send our sympathies to his family. Funeral services for him will take place back in his hometown. For more information call the channel 11 station. Lets see what George has to say about the weather forecast. Tomorrow we are warning everyone to stay in their homes. The ozone will be orange. It's going to be extremely hot tomorrow. If it's not necessary for you to go out, please stay in your homes." the tiny voice warned.

"Officer Dolopis! Can you hear me? Danny, he's not responding!" he yelled from the back. Check to see if he's still breathing!" he instructed, occasionally looking back. Steve placed his ear over his mouth in search of a sound. Nothing. Steve began pressing down on his chest to revive him. He slightly lifted his chin to open his airway. He put his ear over his mouth and nose. "He's fine. He's still breathing." he answered, relieved.

"That's great. You almost scared me back there." Thirty minutes passed.

Officer Dolopis could hear tiny voices fading away. He could feel himself slipping away.

"Ok, we're finally here." Danny exhaled.

"Danny we're losing him again." Steve worried. Steve pressed down on him to revive. He gently lifted his chin and gently blew two breaths into his mouth.

Still Officer Dolopis did not respond.

A beam of light hung over him. It was blinding his view. His mouth was dry. It was cold. He wanted someone to throw a blanket over him. His sight was failing. The only thing he could see was the bright light. He wanted someone to put it out.

"He's barely breathing." Steve sighed.

"What happened? He was fine a minute ago." Danny said, rushing to the back.

He placed his two fingers on the carotid of his cheek for a pulse. "Nothing."

"Quick! Get the defibrillators."

Steve pulled them from the wall and handed them to Danny. He ripped the package open then pulled the back off of the electro pads. He placed them on his chest. "Turn the AED switch on!" he ordered, firmly pressing down on the patient's chest. Officer Dolopis body jumped as each electrical volt traveled through his body but still, he couldn't move. A numb sensation deprived him of each touch. He was feeling lightheaded. His mental capacity had dropped. There was no response.

They looked over at the life line on the screen. It was flat.

"Again!" he ordered, firmly pressing down, shocking him to jump start his heart. Suddenly, the rear doors swung open. A team of doctors had arrived. Steve was relieved.

"We'll take it from here!" one doctor rushed. Breathing heavily, they watched them roll Officer Dolopis off the truck. Officer Dolopis could feel them rolling him into the building. The medical team rushed him into the emergency room.

Moments later, Officer Dolopis woke up gasping for air. He opened his eyes that bright light was still beaming down into his face. He could see a child's face, but hardly transparent. He put his hand up to block the blinding light. "Wake up Mr.! Wake up!" a tiny voice ordered. Officer Dolipis opened his eyes. A child was pushing down on his chest. He found himself stretched out on the ground. He could feel the plush green grass prickling against his skin. Unfamiliar faces surrounded him. "Are you enjoying your visit?" a voice asked. An estranged man held his hand out to help him up. Squinting, Officer Dolopis reached for the hand. Without any effort the man pulled him up. Officer Dolopis could feel himself swiftly jumping to his feet. He weighed every bit of 245 pounds but to him, he felt as light as a feather. It was as if the man had applied too much strength to help him up. Officer Dolopis stared at him. The man's lips were moving but nothing was coming out. He was amazed at the strength of this young man. His palms were soft and warm. The texture of his hand proved he did not engage in physical labor. Officer Dolopis looked around. He noticed the landing pier near the waters. From all directions, people were arriving and leaving by boats. He could see the joy and sorry on their faces as they embraced each other.

"Hi, I'm Officer Dolopis." he smiled, finally introducing himself.

"It's nice to meet you. I will be showing you around during your stay here. Just follow me." the man smiled, with a pleasant voice. At times, Officer Dolopis looked over at the young man. His face was smooth and unblemished. He couldn't quite make out his age. He looked fairly young but sounded old in wisdom. His face was smooth and unblemished. His cold black, thick hair was pulled back into a ponytail. It reached past his hips. He had on an orange shirt with wide knee shorts. Officer Dolopis looked down at his feet. He was bare feet. Surprisingly, they were wholesomely maintained. "By what source could he walk these distant lands and yet, still have beautiful feet?" he thought. From a slight distance, Officer Dolopis noticed a group of men. Lost, they examined their surroundings. They appeared to be newcomers. Harmoniously, they walked in step. Officer Dolopis gradually joined in with them.

"Hello, my name is Sergeant Mathews." one of them said, introducing himself. "And this here is my buddy, Larke. He keeps everybody in good health." he smiled, pointing to his left.

"And my name is Thomas but you can call me Tom. I try to make sure our travel is safe." another man interrupted.

"Hi I'm Kevin." the man from his right, smiled.

"Hi, you can call me Marc. I am the one who accommodates our loved ones with a respectable resting place." another man from behind smiled.

"Nice to meet you all." Officer Dolopis smiled. He stretched his arms out. A sudden change had come over him. A feeling of zest. This was a sensation that he hadn't felt since childhood. He looked down at his hands. He no longer had calluses on the palm of his hands. His skin was creamy smooth. Taking a deep breath, he inhaled the fresh air. He smiled at the sweet fragrances of sprouting nature that filled the air. He was surprised at the sight of seeing so many flowers all in one season. One by one, he examined them. Not one wilted flower could be found. In the fields he could see huge golden sunflowers blazing in the sunlight. Colorful leaves of different shapes and sizes hung in the fair winds. He reached up and caught his hat. A slight breeze had nearly taken it. Confused, he teased his hair. His hair had never felt like this before. It was satin smooth but soft like cotton candy. Butterflies in awesome sizes occasionally crossed his path. The trees were a green he had never seen before. All his life his vision was 20/20, but now, seeing all of this only reveals that his vision was impaired all along. It was as if he was putting on a pair of glasses for the very first time. Back at home, everything had a drab appearance. But here, here everything was in full color. Here, everything was all embracing and made with full potential. Everything that aroused his senses had a cutting-edge as if everything had been made new. He realized that the place he once belonged to, he was truly disabled. Back at home, everything that he touched, tasted, saw, heard or smelled was dull. He was restless. But here . . . here, he was full of energy and spirit. He looked back at the child, wondering if he had seen her some place before. Observing his surroundings, he noticed a huge lofty tree that stood twenty feet high. There was not one bare branch. It was thick with green leaves accompanied by the sound of birds. Just far from the left a child was sitting on its thick branch. Bees fluttered around him like butterflies as he reached his hand into a honeycomb. He managed to get some honey with the tip of his fingers. He plunged them into his mouth to taste it. Honey dripped from the tips of his fingers down to his elbow.

"Somebody quick! Get that kid down! He's going to get attacked by those bees or worse fall from that tree." Officer Dolopis warned.

Mr. Dolopis, relax. He'll be fine." the tour guide smiled. In every direction, every angle, Officer Dolopis could still see people greeting each other with hugs and kisses. At a small distance, he observed a couple reuniting. "I've missed you so much!" the man smiled, lifting a woman into his arms. Teasing his bang, she kissed him on the forehead as she kicked her legs with joy. She hugged him around his neck tightly. Officer Dolopis could see tears of joy in their eyes.

Traveling further, he noticed a young boy riding on the back of a grizzly bear. The child giggled as the bear rolled over, wrestling with him. He rubbed the bear's belly with his tiny fingers. Uncontrollably, he roared with laughter then rubbed his nose into the child's belly, tickling him.

Suddenly, Kevin grabbed hold of a huge fishing net then rushed past Officer Dolopis, almost knocking him down.

"Don't worry son! I'll save you!" he yelled. The boy bounced back onto the bear. Kevin could hear his laughter fade as they ran into the wilderness. In an attempt to chase them, he tripped over a huge mushroom.

"Come back here! I'll make sure you stay in your cage for good this time!" he yelled, after the bear.

"Son he's harmless. Come back here!" the tour guide laughed, waving his arm at him to return.

Astounded at what he had seen, Officer Dolopis did a 360. "Where are we?" he questioned under his breath, looking around.

"You're on a six week vacation. Hurry, I have a lot to show you!" the tour guide continued. He was waiting for Kevin to catch up.

Kevin finally met up with him. Breathing heavily, he stopped to catch his breath. "Drink this before you dehydrate." Larke advised, handing him a canteen of water.

"Thanks." he smiled, graciously gulping it down. Nonstop, he drank. Water gushed from the corners of his mouth. The tour guide headed east first towards the islands. They ventured through various vallies. A vast distance of rushing waters surrounded them. Fresh senses of honeysuckle, berries and spring cucumbers danced in the air. Giant ferns and lush rainforest plants surrounded them. He led them through the cloud-misted rainforest. Officer Dolopis was marveled at the rainbow hues of waterfalls cascading down the majestic mountain cliff. It was absolutely astonishing. This waterfall dropped 80 feet down into the waters. The mountains had green trees and caves surrounded by tropical foliages. The sound of delicate songs of mountain birds echoed from hidden places. The rivers traveled miles ahead. From afar, Officer Dolopis could see people playing in the waters. Scurry waters made him tone deaf. No longer could he hear the tour guide speaking. Only his moving lips could be seen. The edges of the banks were decorated with flowers. Glistening colors of emeralds and stones settled at the bottom. Officer Dolopis kneeled down and put his hand in the cool turquoise waters. Although the traveling waters were rushing, its force was light as a feather. Suddenly, he felt something touch his hand. "What was that?" he whispered, jerking his hand back. Taking a closer look, he spotted it. This was an unusual type of specie. Something that he had never seen before. It was fascinating. It appeared to have blue and green feathers on its back. He leaned forward to get a better view. This fishlike specie slowly traveled into a hidden hole in the side of the mountainous wall. His gaze was suddenly broken. Unaware of where he had landed, he felt something creep across his hands. He quickly looked down. There were an army of ants the size of peanuts crawling all over him. They managed to crawl up his arms. Startled, he jumped to his feet and began dusting them off. Realizing that they were completely harmless, he calmed down. He slowly turned his palms inward and outward as they traveled around his hands. He smiled with amazement. One by one they fell off.

Looking a few feet up ahead, he noticed a man sitting near a huge boat covered with tar. There was a sign nearby. Genesis 6th Avenue lot number 14. There were children surrounding him. He looked young but his charisma revealed that he was much older than he appeared to be. He was accompanied by three other men. Overhearing their conversation, one child asked, "Sir how long did it take you to build this boat?"

"Forty days and forty nights." he answered, delighted.

In disbelief, Officer Dolopis rubbed his eyes. He slowly walked towards him. He could smell a sweet musky odor as he got closer.

Almost like barbeque. Not sure of what to say, he whispered, "Hello Sir is this here your boat?" gently touching it. It was wood sealed with a dark colored tar. He rubbed his hands across the bumpy and hard but slightly sticky texture. Observing its measurements revealed that it was carefully manufactured.

"Why yes son it is." he smiled.

"Hey guys. Come check out this cool boat!" Officer Dolopis hollered, signaling his friends to come over.

Approaching him, they smiled.

"Hi, I'm Kevin. How are you? Kevin smiled, gently shaking his hand.

"Hello."

Kevin kept shaking his hand, not wanting to let it go.

"OK can I have my hand back?" the man smiled.

"Oh sure."

"Do you mind if I take a look inside?" Officer Dolopis continued. His eyes were full of zeal and excitement. This temperament behavior made him look like one of the children.

"Sure, son show this young man around." he grinned, touching his eldest son on the shoulder. Amazed, Officer Dolopis stared into his face then looked over at his father.

"This is your son? The both of you appear to be the same age." he admitted.

"This way." he said, taking the lead. They followed in behind him. Everyone, except Kevin. He wanted to talk to the man that built the boat. Maybe he could get some pointers on animal control," he thought. Meanwhile, Officer Dolopis was taking a look inside. Almost missing his step, he walked into the dim room. Each floor had different compartments. "It's just like the book mentioned." he whispered. Following behind the young man, he ran up to the third floor. Looking up, he discovered a small window in the top of the arched ceiling.

He pushed the window open then peeped his head through the window. "Guys check this out!" he smiled.

"So this is where that bird landed." he continued.

"What bird?" Kevin asked. The man near the boat looked at him. His arms were folded as he shook his head in disbelief. "You don't read much do you?"

"I'm sorry. I don't." he admitted, rubbing the back of his head. He looked up at the small window again.

Sergeant Mathews and the others each took a turn, poking their heads out of the small window.

Boys come on. We have a long day ahead of us!" the tour guide called out.

"Thank you Sir. I wish I could stay a little longer. I had a lot of questions to ask you." Officer Dolopis smiled, rushing off. The tour guide had already gone ahead.

"Nice meeting you." they waved. They finally caught up with the tour guide.

Leading the way, he held up the scroll. He strolled to the left. The climax was getting cooler. They were approaching another island. The waterfall dropped into a deep hallow hole. It's pureness, beauty and tranquility were interrupted only by the sound of waters. There was a stone paved path that ran through the green foliage. The cliffs were painted by flowers and shrubs. On his way to the waterfall, Officer Dolopis could see a giant banyan tree with a trunk so huge not even a wide-angle camera could catch a full view. He frowned. He felt as if he had been deprived of this peace and serenity all his life.

Walking through the vallies, Sergeant Mathews asked, excuse me but where can we go to clean ourselves up?"

"You're looking at it." the tour guide answered, waving his arms over the waters and then pointing to the flowers. Officer Dolopis took advantage of the moment and explored every flower in the vallies. Every flower that he sniffed had it's own frangrance. Traveling a little further, they settled at the base of a spectacular cliff to view the towering waterfall. They could hear the mountain birds.

"And you can eat from every tree of this garden." he suggested, pulling a melon the size of a bowling ball. He broke the straw stem and poked into the fruit.

"Go ahead try one." he smiled, slurping the juice through the straw.

With both hands, Officer Dolopis reached up and pulled one down. Sitting on the ground, under a huge leaf, he bit into it. Juice burst in every direction. It was all over his face. It was a taste he'd never experienced before. It was cold, soft, juicy and sweet. Turning it up, he poured the juice into his mouth.

"This is great!" the others said.

Moments later, a gang of young children ran past them. Then a man along with a woman slowly walked past them. He had a tall thick stick in his hand. There were a herd of sheep following behind him. Sergeant Mathews reached out and touched one of them. "Ba—a—a" it wined. It had a full, white, soft and plush coat.

Officer Dolopis leaned over and whispered, "Is that who I think that is?" in the tour guide's ear.

"Yes it is." he smiled.

"Get out of here."

"Hugh?" he answered, puzzled.

"I . . . mean is that so? Can I meet him?" he asked.

"Sure. Go ahead."

Finding it hard to get up, he reached for one of the leaves. "Excuse me Sir!" he called out.

Stopping, the man turned around. "Yes?"

Officer Dolopis, ran up to him. "You don't know me but I know you. I read about you all the time. I just wanted to say that you're a very faithful and wise man. Because of you, I have stronger faith. And I'm so glad that you got back everything that you lost." he smiled, shaking his hand.

His eyes wailed up with tears. "Oh, thank you son." he smiled.

"Hi it's nice to meet you!" his friends yelled from behind.

"Hello!" he waved back. "Have a good day." he smiled.

"You too."

Officer Dolopis wiped his tears of joy and ran back to finished his meal.

After eating, they walked three more miles. This was unusual for him. Normally he would be exhausted. But he wasn't.

He lifted the little girl upon his shoulders and continued their journey.

The day seemed long before the night fell. Fireflies lit the pathway to guide their steps. Up ahead, they found a spot for lodging and pitched a tent. Officer Dolopis chose to sleep near the end that was half way opened. The sound of crickets plagued the night. Yawning, he lied on his back. He looked up at the blue midnight skies. A full moon accompanied by twinkling stars shed a dim light over his face. He could hear crickets in the night. At night, the river looked completely different. Bright flowers lit the river edges like malibu lights. Sporadic flowers and plants lit the night. Finding it difficult to sleep, he tossed and turned. Occasionally, he could hear voices and water splashing in the night. He raised his head to see where the noise was coming from. He slightly pulled the flap of the tent to take a peek. He could only see a dim figure. He leaned forward to get a better view. Just up ahead, he could see a couple sitting on the banks of the river. They were cuddling and whispering while they dangled their feet in to the moving waters. He could hear the sound of splashing waters. Giggling, they kicked at the neon fish that nipped at the bottom of their feet. Their private conversations remained uninterrupted as harmless mosquitoes floated around them. Children laughed and giggled as they gathered to light a fire camp. He smiled as they danced and played around the burning fire. Suddenly, a swift draft interrupted his moment of peace. It was Sergeant Mathews rushing past him. Officer Dolopis could see the fear in his eyes. Reiterating his past life, he jumped to his feet and dashed through the opening of the tent. From inside, Officer Dolopis could see the movement of his shadow as he searched outside the tent. He spotted an empty bucket just near the water banks. Fearing the onset of a forest fire, he quickly, grabbed it. Panting, he dipped it into the water. Water spilled from the bucket as he clumsily approached the children. "Kids are not suppose to play with fire." he warned, attempting to put it out.

"Mr. Mathews wait!" the tour guide, ordered as he spread his arms out to stop him. "That fire won't harm anyone. It's burn resistant. It only serves as heat to keep you warm."

Sergeant Mathews stopped in his tracks. Puzzled, he scratched his forehead.

The little girl giggled, nonstop.

"Stop that." the tour guide whispered.

"I can't. It's just too funny."

"Sh-sh. Go to sleep or you're not going to get any special treats tomorrow."

"Aw alright." she pouted. She laid her head on her pillow. Giggling, she pulled the covers over her head to hide her laughter. It was no use. The tour guide could still hear her. Sighing with frustration, he stepped out for a moment. Sergeant Mathews managed to settle down and returned to his resting place. Finally, everyone was fast asleep. Moments later, the sound of voices awaken Officer Dolopis. Still half asleep he raised his head. From a distance he could see the tour guide standing before a burning fire. He couldn't make out what was burning. Unsure of what was happening, he laid his head back down. One night of excitement was enough for him. "Maybe he's trying to keep warm." he thought to himself. Nonchalant, he closed his eyes and went back to sleep.

After a long nights rest the guys got up and began gathering their belongings. Officer Dolopis was still asleep. He rolled over on his side. He could hear the sound of voices and things being shifted around. He opened his eyes. Larke and Sergeant Mathews were folding their cots and sleeping bags.

"Good morning Mr. Dolopis." the little girl smiled. "You want to go with me to gather some berries?" she continued.

"Sure." he smiled, rubbing his tired eyes. He stretched for a moment then slowly got up. He rolled up his sleeping bag and tucked his cot away.

Good morning." Marc smiled. He was folding his clothes and putting them away.

"Morning." he answered, peeping through the crack of the tent. He could see the tour guide picking up stones.

"What's he doing?"

"He said he was going out to get water." Marc answered.

Officer Dolopis shook his head in confusion.

Marc shrugged his shoulders. He was just as confused.

"We'll be back. We're going out for some food." Officer Dolopis sighed. He lowered his head to exit the tent.

"Alright. Just don't go too far. We'll be ready to leave soon." he advised.

Officer Dolopis grabbed hold of the child's hand and picked up a basket. The child led the way as they traveled the distant path. Slowly, he walked with his hands in his pockets. He whistled a tune to sooth his ears.

"Slow down." he finally suggested to the child. He picked up his speed to catch up with her. They were getting close. He could see it just up ahead. It was beautiful. The naturalized planting of the trees and shrubs lined the gently curving path which lead to the garden. The highly sweet aroma of olive plants beckoned him to enter. Making his entry, blossoms and shades of cream, white, yellow and orange protruded from the trees that surrounded him. There were trees full of fruit and all types of vegetables. There were beans, broccoli, and corn sprouting. Carrots, potatoes, and tomatoes coming from all directions. He dropped the basket nearby. He lifted the child upon his shoulders and stood underneath one. She reached up and pulled a plum, tossing it into the basket.

"There's one over there." she said, pointing. He leaned closer for her. "I got it." she said, pulling an apple. Suddenly, Officer Dolopis heard distant voices then a loud roar.

"Quick, there's a mango over to the left." the child suggested.

"Sh-sh." he whispered, putting her down.

"What's wrong?"

"I thought I heard something."

"Roar!" There it is again. It sounded like it was coming from over there." he whispered.

He gently grabbed the child's hand then moved closer. From behind a bush, he could slightly see a man. He spread the twigs apart to get a better view. From a distance he could see a huge stout man circling around this large fierce lion. Officer Dolopis watched him as he stood still in one position, ready. His knees and arms were bent, ready to make his move. His muscles were well defined. Every movement he made flexed a muscle.

Finally making his move, he grabbed hold of the lion. The lion, nearly his height, stood tall on his hind legs, tussling. Officer Dolopis could see minor scratches on his arms as he tangled with this lion face to face. He managed to maneuver his way behind the lion. He eased his arms underneath the lions arm pits. He positioned his arms over the back of his neck and clamped his fingers. In a tight grip, he held the lion in a headlock. Occasionally, he pressed his head downward to get him to calm down. "Roar!" The lion got louder. Officer Dolopis was mesmerized. He wished Kevin could be there to witness. Watching them tangled up was like watching two siblings.

"Honey will you please leave that lion alone and let me finish braiding your hair." a woman interrupted. She was sitting on the porch between two pillars.

Laughing, he let him loose. Disappointed, the lion took his place underneath a tree. Resting, he licked his paws.

"I won again. Maybe next time Teddy." he teased, taking his seat before the woman.

Breathing heavily, he leaned back on the woman to rest. His caramel skin tone shimmered from the sunlight. His cold black hair was partially braided on one side.

She smoothed out his soft, silky hair with the palms of her hands. Gently, she began combing through his long thick locks. "Sam your hair is so beautiful." she smiled.

"Please don't get it cut. What if you fall weak? You won't be able to help me with the lumber around here." she pleaded.

"Sweetheart, we've had this conversation before. I promise I'll be fine. Alright?" he said, assuring her with a kiss on the hand.

"Now let me get back to work. I have to replant some of these trees. Officer Dolopis was still watching from behind. His mouth fell open as he watched this heavy-duty vigorous man wrap his massive arms around this oak tree and lift it. He carried it over into the garden. "Mankind sure can ruin some things." he complained, planting it in it's original place. Officer Dolopis was astounded.

"What happened Mr. Dolopis? What did you see?" the child asked, pulling at his shirt. Officer Dolopis was speechless.

"Mr. Dolopis you're scaring me. Say something." she whimpered.

"Hugh?" he answered, finally breaking from his fascination.

"What happened?" she continued.

"Oh, nothing. Let's go." he ordered, grabbing the fruit basket then pulling her along. Still looking behind he rushed back to the others. By then the tour guide had returned. They were all sitting around eating while the tour guide entertained them with adventurous stories. Officer Dolopis sat down to join them. He looked over at his friends. They were hanging on to his every word. He had some exciting stories to share too but he didn't want to steal the spotlight. He enjoyed seeing their faces light up when the tour guide told them stories. Sergeant Mathews passed him a bowl of rolls. He put his hand up and shook his head no. He didn't have much of an appetite. He kept thinking about the man he saw back in the garden. He wondered how such a man was capable of having that kind of strength.

"Is everything alright son?" the tour guide asked, interrupting his thoughts.

"Oh, yeah sure." he admitted, trying to focus on his stories. After breakfast, they packed up their things and continued their journey.

"We're going to head south. They walked for miles site seeing. The sun lit up the entire forest. Marc and Officer Dolopis walked side by side, talking. The others were far up ahead. Officer Dolopis suddenly, stopped in his tracks.

"What's the matter?" Marc asked.

"Did you hear that?

"Hear what?"

"I heard someone giggling. It sounded like it was coming from over there."

"Man I think you been out in these woods too long. Come on lets go catch up with the others." He suggested.

"I'll be there in a second."

"Alright." He answered, still feeling uneasy. He rushed ahead to catch up with the others.

Officer Dolopis heard the giggling again. He got a little closer and stood behind a tree. Just intervals away he could see someone stretched out on an armless sofa near a water fountain. Women surrounding him with flowers and treats blocked his view. He could only see a man's toes wiggling. "David sit still." the woman said, sitting on the end massaging his feet.

"Oh David you're so funny." One girl giggled, feeding him a grape. There was another woman standing. She was fanning him with a huge leaf that she had threaded into a fan. Moving closer, Officer Dolopis stepped on a twig.

"Jonathon did you hear that? David asked.

"I didn't hear anything." he smiled. His eyes were closed with pleasure. So consumed with the massages he didn't bother to look. He lay stretched out on his belly on a chase while the woman caressed his bulk shoulders. There were women surrounding him with oils and perfumes. Another stood over him with a huge umbrella while the other fanned him to keep him cool.

"Right there. Now move over to the left side." he instructed his massager.

Who's there? Show your face!" David continued.

"David it's nothing. Lay still. You're going to mess up your manicure." another girl said, filing his finger nail.

Giggling, Officer Dolopis tip-toed his way back to join the others. Walking along, he could see chimpanzees swinging from branch to branch. One little boy sat underneath a huge tree reading a book. He was holding a baby chimpanzee on his lap. The chimp was clothed with a tropical shirt and shorts. Officer Dolopis watched them as the chimp attempted to give the boy a bite of his banana. Refusing it, the boy pushed his hand away. The chimp bounced on his leg making a loud noise at his refusal. Making another attempt, he shoved it in his face. "No, I don't want any." the boy refused.

Upset, the chimp bounced on his leg, crying. He tried once more. The boy refused. Finally, the chimp got up and walked away. Officer Dolopis laughed as he passed them up. He finally caught up with Marc. They walked ahead as the tour guide led the way. Moments later, they heard a voice from behind. They peeped through the tree branches. There was a man standing alone having a conversation. He was picking apples and tossing them into the basket. "Ok but what if there were five good apples out of fifty rotten ones. Do I need to throw all the apples away and waste the five good ones or do I only need to get rid of all the rotten ones." he questioned, getting further away. "Alright, well let's say there were sixty rotten apples and only ten good ones. Should I reserve the ten good ones or throw all of them away. Or maybe if there were eighty rotten apples and fifteen good ones. Do I keep the fifteen good ones or just get rid of all the apples. But if . . . ." he continued, picking apples and walking away.

"Who is he talking to? Marc asked, nudging Officer Dolopis.

"I'm not sure."

They watched him do this until they could no longer see him.

They continued walking. He could still see the tour guide and the others. They carried on with their journey. They walked a little further and found a resting place.

They found a huge tree and decided to sit underneath it. Finding a spot, Officer Dolopis laid on his back. Ordinarily, he would have taken advantage of this occasion and taken a nap. But he wasn't restless. He looked up at the skies. It was a blue that he had never seen before. Birds and eagles danced in the skies. Changing his position, he laid his cheek up against the grass. It was plush and prickly against his face. The grass was a pure green. Normally it would itch and flare up his allergies but it didn't. It was pollen free. He could never do this back at home. Not wanting this moment of beauty to escape him, he rolled around in the grass. He was breathing heavily but never exhausted. He inhaled to catch another fragrance. He rolled on his back with his hands folded behind his head. Looking over at Marc, he smiled. He was stretched out on a hammock. He watched him swing to and fro. Smiling, Officer Dolopis closed his eyes with satisfaction. Half asleep, he could see the little girl swinging on the rope of a cobra as it wrapped it's ends around a tree branch. Finally, he dosed off to the sound of chirping birds that surrounded them. The others laid underneath the tree and fell asleep too. Sleep became seconds, seconds became minutes and minutes became hours. From a distance, a kitten laid stretched out on the porch. Undisturbed, the cat licked it's paws as a mouse went back and forth across it's back. The sound of child's play filled Officer Dolopis' eardrums. A soldier of ants traveled across a toddlers legs as she pulled mini flowers from the ground. Not wanting to wake up from his dreams, he tossed and turned. It was still daylight when he and his friends woke up. After collecting their items they began walking. From a distance, he could see a group sitting on a bench. They were gathered around a man sitting on the table. He appeared to be some sort of teacher. He held up his scroll. Reading and pointing, he gave instructions. Walking a little further, he noticed people of all ages, colors and nationalities standing in a long line in front of a billboard. He moved closer to take a look. There was a roster posted on the bill board. It was labeled Promise Land with a long list of names. He could see them searching the roster for their loved ones. Some had gifts in their hands and some had the things they remembered doing with their loved ones. One boy had a chessboard folded underneath his arm as he peeped his head around the tall person in front of him. A three year old little girl had her favorite book in her hand. There was a man with a saxophone. Another man awaited with flowers. One lady had a sweater that she knitted. Looking further down, he could see an elderly couple nervously waiting with a blue knitted hat and bootie. Some left with tears of joy on their faces and some were disappointment. Across the way, he noticed a line of people with different ailments. One by one, each person got over their infirmaries. One man slowly lifted himself from a wheelchair then started walking. An assistant stepped up and took it, tossing it in a pile of various medical equipment, artillery and vehicles. A welder was sitting before the pile melting everything into pots and pans. One lady took off her glasses and tossed them into the pile. Looking towards the end of the line, he noticed a man removing his sunglasses. He kneeled down to remove the straps from his dog and set him free. His eyes opened with amazement as he watched an elderly lady slowly transform back to her youth. The strings of her salt and pepper hair slowly changed to full colored black. The hump in her back slowly disappeared as her posture straightened. The wrinkles in her face, neck and hands gradually went smooth. Her weak, jagged voice became strong and soft. Her weak vision was transformed to perfection. Her pale complexion reverted to it's tender tone. Her teeth were once again pearly white.

"Come on Mr. Dolopis. Lets go." a tiny voice spoke, grabbing him by the finger than pulling him away. Officer Dolopis looked down. It was his little friend who met him at the beginning of his journey.

"You want to see my bubbles?" she asked.

"Yes, let me see your bubbles." he smiled. She blew forth a cluster of bubbles. She giggled as he attempted to bust them.

"Here, do it again." she giggled, blowing forth some more.

Finally, he lifted her on his shoulders and headed back to find the others. Retracing his steps, he caught up with Marc. He was picking tulips from a nearby tree. Distracted by the long stem tulips, he had fallen behind. "Ooh tulips!" the little girl smiled, reaching to get down. Officer Dolopis gently put her down. She ran over and picked a few.

"This one is for you." she smiled, handing one to Officer Dolopis.

"Thank you Sweetie."

She ran up ahead to catch up with the tour guide.

"Who are those for?" Officer Dolopis finally asked, teasing Marc.

"These are for my grandmother."

"I didn't know she was here. Where is she?" he asked, smiling.

"My grandmother's deceased." he answered, rearranging the bouquet to his delight. The air was saturated with the fragrance of nectar. He ran to catch up with the rest of the group. The tour guide and the others were resting under a shed. "Hey Mister! Is there a graveyard around here?" he called out. Finally reaching them, he stopped to catch his breath.

The tour guide didn't answer right away. He was reading the scroll.

Nonchalant, he answered, "No. Why do we need a graveyard?" without looking up.

"We need a place to bury our dead loved ones." he answered, disturbed.

Still looking over the scroll, the tour guide replied, "There's no need. Everyone here is alive."

"You mean . . . she—e's alive?" Marc reluctantly asked. His racing heart feared the tour guide's answer. Everyone got silent. Awaiting his answer, the men surrounded him.

"You can find your grandmother over there." he answered, pointing at a long line. Marc turned his head in that direction. He could see a man picking up his son. He was crying and laughing. They were so happy to see each other.

He looked over at the tour guide. He was still reading and looking at some building plans. Marc wondered if he had family too. He glanced over at Sergeant Mathews. He was down by the river cooling off. Sergeant Mathews smiled as he wiggled his toes into the cool waters. A gentle touch, approached him from behind. "Son is that you?" a gentle sweet voice questioned. Recognizing her scent, he turned around. "Mama? Is that really you?" he asked. Amazed, he stood up. "You look so young. I almost didn't recognize you."

"Oh my baby! How have you been?" she asked, hugging him. Lifting her up, he spins her around. "Mama. I've missed you so much!" he cried. "You have two grand children. Their names are Micheal and Kaytlin." Touched, she places her hand on her chest. My son looks just like papa. Where is papa?" he asked, looking around.

"He's right over here." she answered, leading him down a dirt path. "Son! My boy!" his father cried out. He lifted his son and spinned him around. I'm so proud of you. My boy became a firefighter. Who would have ever guessed? You used your time doing good deeds.

Crying, Officer Dolopis and Marc watched them from a distance as they reunited. They slowly disappeared as they reached the top of the hill. "I'm really happy for Sergeant Mathews." Officer Dolopis smiled.

"Margaret come on. We're going to be late!" a voice called, interrupting Marc's thoughts.

"That name sounds familiar." Marc thought. Overlooking Officer Dolopis' statement, Marc looked past him. From behind, Marc could see two women rushing to get to a boat. In a hurry, she dropped an earring.

"Oh, wait Barbara. I dropped my earring." she said, kneeling down. She spread her hands out on the ground, in search of it.

"Just forget about it. You can always get another pair. Let's go before they leave us."

"I can't. Harold brought these earrings for me on our first date." she worried. Marc's wide eyes teared up. He took a deep swallow. Surpassing his friends, he slowly walked away. Officer Dolopis and the others got quiet as they watched their friend depart from them.

"Marc is there something wrong?" Officer Dolopis asked, concerned. He didn't answer.

From a distance, Marc spotted the earring. He kneeled down to pick it up. "Is this it?" he asked, approaching Margaret from behind.

By then he was crying. She turned around. "Oh, yes! Thank you." she answered, reaching for it.

Still holding it, he stared into her deep brown eyes. Her skin was a smooth dark brown. He noticed her beauty mark on her left cheek. She still looked like herself, only younger. She was beautiful.

Coming closer, she asked, "Is everything alright Harold?"

"It's me grandma!" Marc cried.

"Marc?" she cried, touching his face. "Oh my God! It's really you! You look just like your grandpa! she cried, hugging and kissing him. Her honeysuckle hair trickled against his cheek. Almost forgetting, he tearfully smiled, "Here, these are for you." He handed her the tulips.

"I've missed you so much!" she smiled, taking them. "How's your mother? Is everything fine back at home? Come on, I can't wait to tell your grandpa! Harold!" she carried on, pulling Marc by the arm.

From a distance, Officer Dolopis watched them as they got on the boat. He wiped a tear with is thumb as he watched the boat leave.

Suddenly, the clapping thunder roared. He looked up. The sky turned grey. The clouds were starting to close in. The winds were high. Rain started pouring down. Officer Dolopis grabbed hold of a huge leaf. Running, he covered his head with it. Clattering rain tapped on the surface of the leaf as he ran for cover.

"Quick, everybody find shelter. It looks like there's going to be a bad storm!" warned Tom. He pulled his jacket over his head as he ran towards the shed. The tour guide was sitting on a pillow near a burning fire, reading. There were knee level tables decorated with strawberries, blueberries, apples and pears nearby. There was another table covered with all types of drinks. The table across had homemade pies and bread. The aroma of fresh bakery filled the room.

"There's no bad storm coming. Its only rain." the tour guide said, biting into an apple.

"I've been studying weather for thirty-two years. I think I know what I'm talking about." Tom answered.

"And I've lived here for over 1600 years and I tell you there's no storm. Because there's never been a storm here before." he chewed.

Bewildered, Tom stared at him.

Grabbing a pillow, the three of them gathered around him. They ate and laughed at the stories he told them. They spent the rest of the evening talking. After the rain settled down they continued their mission. Up ahead Officer Dolopis could see two women feuding. Passing them up, he overheard their conversation.

"Jacob will be here next month and you've ruined my dress. This is why I don't like you wearing my stuff." Rachel complained.

"It's not my fault. How was I suppose to know that it would rip so easily? I only wore it once." Rebecca answered.

"Girls please don't fight. Rachel I'll have another one made for you." their father interrupted. His arms were full of logs. He tossed them into a pile.

"Thank you daddy." she smiled, kissing him on the cheek.

"Is supper ready. I've had a long day and I'm hungry." he complained.

Officer Dolopis and Larke looked at each other then grinned as they passed them up. They traveled the mountains and the allies. Soon they arrived to another island. They stopped near the water. One by one, they dipped into the waters. Officer Dolopis kneeled down to take a drink. He splashed his face with both palms full of water.

He looked over at Tom. He was throwing rocks across the river. He looked uneasy.

Officer Dolopis looked back at Larke for an answer.

He shrugged his shoulders without saying anything.

"Is everything alright?" Officer Dolopis asked, slowly approaching him.

"Yeah. It's just that I left a lot of unfinished business back at home." he complained.

"What do you mean?" Larke asked

"I was in my last term with college. My marriage was suppose to take place next month."

"You were engaged?" Officer Dolopis asked, excited.

"Yeah. Her name was Serina Montego. We planned on having two children." He looked down at the ground.

"The last thing I said to her was that I didn't like those colors. We were shopping for furniture. I know she's worried about me. I just wish I could have gotten the chance to say good bye or something." he gasped, teary eyed.

"I'm sure she's fine. It's just going to take some time for her but she'll be fine." Officer Dolopis consoled.

In deep thought, he watched the rock skip across the waters.

"Come on lets go grab a bite to eat." Officer Dolopis suggested, patting him on the back.

Larke smiled with approval.

Throwing his last rock, he turned to join them.

"Ouch!" a voice bellowed.

Tom turned around. He noticed a young lady pulling her legs from the water. She was dripping wet. She had a slight cut on her calf. It was bleeding.

"What happened!" her friends asked, assisting her as she hopped to find a seat.

"I don't know. I think something bit me." she answered in disbelief.

"That's not possible. There's nothing harmful in these waters."

"I am so sorry!" Tom nervously interrupted. By then he was rushing around to the other side of the waters. Larke followed behind him. Officer Dolopis slowly followed them.

"Let me take a look. I do this for a living." Larke said, kneeling down. He gently took her leg.

"I'm so sorry. It was an accident. I was throwing rocks and . . . ." Tom tried to explain.

"You were throwing rocks!" she interrupted.

"Do you know you could have put someone's eye out by throwing rocks." she scorned.

"I wasn't thinking. I'm really sorry. How can I make this up to you." he pleaded.

"You can't! I have a soccer game coming up. Now I won't be able to play." she complained. "

My name is Mrs. Slovichia and this here is my daughter, Corina." her mother interrupted, introducing herself to Tom.

"Here, try this." Mrs. Slovichia suggested, handing Larke a huge olive leaf.

"What's this?" he asked, puzzled.

"Just wrap it around her leg. It will be fine in a couple of days."

"But what if it gets infected." he asked, worried.

"It won't. No one here can get an infection."

She got up to check on her meal.

"Mam, I'm so sorry. How can I make this up to your daughter?" Tom pleaded, following her into the house.

"Hand me those herbs over there." she ordered.

"Do you all need anything?" he asked, handing the bowl to her.

"Yes, you can start by eating with us. We can discuss it over supper." she suggested.

Almost knocking a chair over, he shook his head in agreement.

"Be back here at 7:30." she smiled.

"Yes mam." he answered, nervously exiting her home.

He waved goodbye to the young lady.

She turned her head away with displeasure.

"What happened?" his friends asked, rushing to his side.

"Her mom wants me to come back for supper."

"That's great!" they whispered.

They could hear the lady calling for the girl.

"Corina dear, come taste this and tell me what you think."

He turned around once more to steal a look at her.

"Coming mother!" she answered, beaming at him.

She slowly got up and limped into the house.

"Hugh!" The nerve of him." she uttered, slamming the door behind her.

He turned around to conceal his laughter.

"Man, she is really hot at you." Larke grinned.

"Yeah, I saw that icy look she gave you." Officer Dolopis added.

"What am I going to do? I have to play soccer." Tom teased, mocking her.

"I hope everything work out for you with supper." Officer Dolopis sympathized.

"What do you mean? You guys are coming too." he said, pulling a fruit from a nearby branch. He bit into it. It was sweet and cool. Juice dripped down his lips.

"Naw, not this time. I'll wait till everything cools down." Larke answered.

"That's just great. I thought you two were my friends."

"We are. You're the one who decided to throw rocks." Larke grinned.

"That's not fair. You know that was an accident."

"Are you sure? I mean she was real cute and now you're going over for supper." Officer Dopolis teased.

"Now it's not even like that."

"He does have a point." Larke joined in.

"Why you little . . . ." he said, throwing his fruit at Larke.

Larke ducked behind a tree.

"Careful, that's how you got in trouble the last time. You might hit another beauty." Officer Dolopis teased.

"I'll get you yet." he said, chasing after Officer Dolopis. Laughing, they ran from tree to tree. When they returned, the tour guide was helping a lady plant trees. Tom went inside to freshen up. Hours later, he returned to the young lady's home. The room was silent for a moment. He nervously tucked his napkin in his shirt. He took a bite. Without chewing, he took a deep swallow. "Your cooking is fascinating Mrs. Slovichia." he smiled, breaking the silence. Still no one said anything. "So how's the leg?" he finally, asked Corina.

She squinted her eyes at him with disapproval.

"Don't mind her. She's just upset because she could not play soccer this evening." Mrs. Slovichia answered.

"I'm sorry you missed the game." he softly said.

Still she was quiet.

"I wish there was some kind of way to make it up to you."

"Do you know how to play soccer?" she asked, sarcastically.

"Yes, as a matter of fact I do."

A smile suddenly came across her lips. The glow in her eyes revealed what she was thinking.

"No, I'm not going to play with a bunch of women." he replied.

"Aw, come on. If it had not been for you I wouldn't have missed the game."

"Yes, I know but . . . ."

"And you did say that if there was anything you could do to help you would." her mother, interrupted.

"Yeah, but Mrs. Slovichia these are women." he complained.

"Do these women intimidate you or something?" Corina teased.

"No but . . . ."

"Then what's the problem?" she continued, staring at him.

Those beautiful eyes pierced his soul. He was unable to refuse. "Ok, I'll do it." he finally answered, giving in.

"Great! The next game we have is six days from now. It starts at 8 p.m. So don't be late." she chattered.

"And Corina's going to need your help around the house. She feeds the chickens and horses every morning so you're going to need to stack the hay. The milk and the fruit in the back yard is collected. on Thursdays.

"You might need to write this down." Corina joined.

"Here." Corina smiled, handing him a pen and notepad.

And she does the laundry and gathers eggs from the barn on Fridays.

"Mmm, not to mention the game is coming up this Saturday." she mumbled with a mouth full of food.

And she also refills the pitchers with water on Fridays. Corina will show you everything." her mother continued.

He slowly chewed his meal as she carried on with Corina's weekly chores. He no longer enjoyed his meal. It suddenly became bitter. As time passed, he felt more comfortable. They laughed and talked over supper.

He looked down at his watch. "It's getting late. I really enjoyed this meal but I have to get going. I have a long day ahead of me tomorrow." he sighed, staring at Corina.

Looking down at her plate, she grinned.

Mrs. Slovichia stood up to clear the table.

"Well it was certainly a pleasure having you here for supper. We'll have to do this again." she smiled. She looked over at Corina with approval.

"I look forward to it."

"Corina could you walk Tom to the door." she suggested, still eyeing her.

"Sure." she answered, warning her to behave. Giving her mother faces, she followed behind him.

"Well I'll see you tomorrow morning." he turned and smiled.

"Ok and don't be late."

"I won't. Goodnight." he smiled.

"Goodnight." She stood there until he was no longer in view then closed the door.

Everyone was already in bed when he arrived home. He could see that Officer Dolopis and Larke were fast asleep. He tiptoed to the drawer and pulled out his pajamas. Stepping behind the screen, he threw them on. He slowly tiptoed to his bed and pulled the blanket back. Fluffing his pillow, he got into bed.

"So Tom . . . How was dinner." Officer Dolopis asked. He looked over at him. He was sitting up in bed and Larke was sitting across from him in his bed. They eagerly waited for his response.

"I thought you two were asleep." he grinned.

"We decided to wait up." Larke teased.

"Well?"

"Well what?" Tom said, shrugging his shoulders.

"How was dinner?"

"It was fine?"

"That's it? Just fine?" Lark continued.

"What do you want me to say?"

"How was dinner with Corina?" he sighed.

"Oh it was alright." he grinned.

"You like her. Don't you?" Officer Dolopis accused.

"She's alright." he shyly smiled.

"She's more than alright. You want to marry her don't you?" they teased, throwing pillows at him.

'Guys knock if off! I need my rest." he said, fluffing his pillow. He lay down.

"I have a long day ahead of me tomorrow." he smiled, trying to be serious.

"Oh yeah that's right. He has to help Corina tomorrow." they teased.

Rising up once more, he said, "Guys I can't sleep. Keep it down."

"Hey Dolopis I guess we're being too loud. He needs his rest. He's got a long day tomorrow with Corina."

"Yeah, he's such a romance. They'll be picking fruit and flowers together." Dolopis teased.

Tom pulled a pillow from underneath and without looking, threw it at him. He laid his head back down, nonchalantly closing his eyes.

They giggled in the night as Tom dosed off to sleep.

The next morning. He looked over at the clock. It had passed the hour. Hastily, he got up out of bed. He got fully dressed and ran down stairs.

"Good morning. Good bye." he said, rushing past his friends.

"Hey aren't you going to eat breakfast?" the tour guide asked, passing a plate to Larke.

"Not right now. I'm running late. I have to help Corina." he said, reaching for the door.

"Talk to you later." he said, rushing off.

He ran past the hills and mountains. He finally reached Corina's house.

"You're late." she said, swinging on the porch with her leg stretched out on a bench stool.

"I know. I'm sorry. I got a late start." he confessed.

"It's alright." she smiled.

"Ok where do I start?" he asked, breaking his gaze.

"Over there, she said, pointing to a nearby barn. She limped as she lead the way. She slowly opened one of the stables, "Here is where you will milk the cows. There were eight cows standing around eating hay. We get six gallons of milk from each cow once a day. Each cow has a number around their neck. Doing this can help you keep track of which one is next in line to give milk.

"This here is Zoo." she said, patting her on the head. There was a number one stamped on her bell. It's her turn to produce milk." she said, reaching for her bell. "Be sure to sit on the same side at the same time. She's use to this routine. Zoo meet Tom. He'll be getting milk from you today. Are you going to be nice today? she smiled, speaking in a baby-like tone. There's a bucket over there. You can fill it up six times. Then pour it into that milk storage container sitting on that huge wheel barrow. Once you're done, you can push it over into our freezing room. Limping, she led him to the underground basement. He hastily grabbed hold of the double doors as she attempted to pull. "This here is our freezing room. It's very cold down there so be careful not to get locked in. Sometimes it gets stuck. Always leave the doors open until you're finished." she suggested. After you're done I'll show you where to gather the fruit. Call me if you need anything." she smiled. He watched her as she limped over to the front porch. She sat there quietly thumbing through a magazine. Grabbing a wooden stool, he sat down and placed the bucket underneath the cow. He reached underneath the cow and began washing it's udder with a warm wash cloth than gently began pulling. Milk began squirting into the bucket. One by one, he began milking the cows. Occasionally, Corina looked up at him. After completing his task, he poured the buckets of milk into the container then pulled it into the basement.

"Ok all set." he smiled.

Closing her book, she stood up to pour him a cold glass of tea. "You did a great job. Now why don't you take a break? I made some snacks," she smiled, filling his glass.

"Thank you."

They laughed and talked as time passed.

"Ok, I have to get back to work." he said, taking his last sip.

"I'll show you where we gather the fruit." She stood up and guided him to the back of the house. This is where we pick our fruit." she said, pulling a banana from a tree. The banana was fifteen inches long and six inches wide. One by one, she grabbed one and put it into her basket. He pushed the wheel barrow closer to her. It took two hours to gather them. They managed to gather all the ripe fruit. "You can pull this out around to the front. I'm going to fix us a snack." she suggested, wiping the sweat from her forehead.

"Alright." he smiled. He pulled the barrow around to the front of the house.

"Alright, I brought some fresh fruit, water, and peanut butter and jelly sandwiches." she announced, coming out the front door. I hope you know how to play spades because I brought some cards."

"Do I know how to play spades? Now come on now." he bragged.

"I'll deal." she called, taking a bite into her sandwich. She dealt the cards and sorted the cards in her hands. She knew she had a losing hand but she was going to bluff her way out of it. Tom already knew what she was up to. He purposely threw out a losing card so that she would win.

"Is that all you had?" she asked, pulling the cards from the center.

"It's my strategy." he grinned.

"More like tragedy." she teased. "Hey after this do you want to practice for the game?" she continued.

"Well, I don't really know how to play." he admitted.

"That's why I said practice silly." she grinned, grabbing a ball.

"Uh, I don't know." he said, still hesitant.

"Come on. It's not that difficult." she said, grabbing his hand.

He looked down at her hand holding his. Her soft and silky hands convinced him to say yes.

"Ok, this is where you should stand." she suggested, positioning him. "I'll bounce the ball off my head and when it comes to you hit it with any part of your body except your elbows or hands." she instructed. She bounced the ball with the forefront of her head. He returned it by kicking it. He watched her as she skillfully maneuvered her one foot to return the ball. From every angle she returned the ball. He was impressed. Back and forth, they passed the ball. Catching on, he managed to sneak the ball past her.

"Great job." she smiled. The ball was under control for a moment then finally bounced into the field.

"Alright. I think that's enough practice for today. You're a fast learner." she breathed.

"I still have a hard time with that knee action."

"You'll get it after a few days." she answered.

He looked up at the sky. The night was starting to fall. "I guess I'll be leaving now. It's getting kind of late." he said, slowly turning away.

"Alright." she said, disappointed,

"Hey Tom."

"Yes?" he answered, turning around.

"I'll see you tomorrow." she smiled, tossing him a peach.

He quickly reached up and caught it.

"Sure thing."

She limped onto the porch and went into the house. Smiling, she slowly closed the door behind her. "Good night mom." she shouted from the kitchen.

"Good night."

Corina limped towards her bedroom. Gently, she closed the bedroom door. She leaned back against the door and smiled for a moment. The thought of Tom made her giggle. She realized that he was really a nice person. Humming, she walked into the bathroom. An hour later, she came out in her satin silk PJs. Her shoulder length hair was damp. Still humming, she twisted her hair in a towel to dry it. She turned the light switch out and tucked herself into bed. She laid there staring at the moon as it changed shapes then finally closed her eyes. The next morning, the sound of chickens woke her up. She peeped through the blinds. It was Tom. He had gotten up early enough to feed the chickens. Realizing the time, she got up and changed her clothes. She could smell hot cakes as she got closer to the kitchen. There was a bundle of eggs sitting on the counter.

"Good morning, mom." she said, kissing her on the cheek.

"Oh, good morning Sweetie."

"You need me to help you with anything mom?" she asked.

"No just go out there and tell that young man to come in and eat some breakfast."

"Alright."

Stretching she slowly stepped out onto the porch. She could see Tom from a distance carrying a bundle of hay on his back.

"Tom!" she called out. He could see her waving her arms, signaling him to come over.

"My mom wants you to come in for breakfast!" she continued.

He gently placed the hay down and ran into the house.

"Good morning." he smiled, grabbing a seat.

"Good morning."

"I see you got here early today." Corina smiled.

"I thought that I would make up for yesterday."

"So are you almost done feeding the horses?" Mrs. Slovichia asked.

"Yes mam. I'm just bundling the hay now."

"I'm impressed." Corina smiled.

"Well do you think you'll be up for some soccer later? The big day is tomorrow."

"Sure."

"Great." she smiled.

"How's your ankle?"

"Better but not well enough to play. So are you going to invite your friends and family to the game?"

"Sure."

"I bet your girlfriend will be proud to know that you are learning to play soccer." she ease dropped.

"I'm not so sure about that. Hey . . . I'm gonna go finish up with this hay." he uttered. He had a disturbed look on his face.

"I'm sorry. Did I say something wrong?" she asked, concerned.

"No. It's just that I've got a lot to do that's all." he answered, nervously, getting up from the table.

He slowly pushed the chair underneath the table then walked out. Corina and her mother looked at each other. From a distance, Corina could see him lifting loads of hay then bundling them up.

"Mom I'm going to go finish the laundry." she said, still in deep thought.

Alright, but what about your breakfast. Aren't you going to finish eating?" she asked.

"I'm not that hungry. I have to get those clothes off the line. So I can hang some more."

"All right." she said, drying the dishes.

She grabbed a basket full of damp clothes along with an empty one then walked out of the house.

For every piece of clothe she pulled off the line, she replaced. Occasionally, she'd look over at Tom. He was working hard. He looked as if he had a lot on his mind. She wanted to know and she was sure to find out. She threw a blanket on the line. Then pulled a blouse off the line. Folding it, she shouted, "Are you still up for soccer!"

"Sure."

"Well I'm going to go put these clothes away then I'll be out." She lifted the basket of clothes and carried it into the house.

"Ok you're ready?" she smiled, grabbing the ball. "Ready as I'll ever be." he answered, slowly approaching her.

"Now show me what you remember." she said, passing him the ball. He bounced it from one foot to another then to his head springing it back to her.

"Nice." she smiled. She repeated the same moves then rotated it back to him.

"I see you're using your other foot more." he observed.

"It's fine just as long as I stay in one spot. Now let me see you travel with the ball." she instructed.

Rolling the ball from foot to foot, he ran across the field.

"That's great. Now pass it to me."

He maneuvered the ball from his foot to his forehead then passed it over.

"Good job." she said, catching it. "So you think you're ready?" she asked, walking along side him.

"I think I am."

"Ok you two, It's time for supper." her mother interrupted, peeping her head out of the door. Tom looked at Corina with puzzled eyes. He worried that she would ask more questions about his fiancé.

"I would stay for supper but I've gotta get going." he responded, hastily.

"OK, but be back here at 10 a.m. for practice. The game is tomorrow evening and I want to make sure you're ready." she warned.

"Sure thing. I'll see you soon. Bye." he smiled, leaving.

"Later." she waved. She tossed the ball in the yard. Her mother smiled at her as she walked into the house.

"What?" she uttered, pulling a chair out to take a seat.

"Nothing."

"Why are you smiling mom." she asked.

"You like him don't you?" she teased.

"No mom. We are just friends." she sighed.

"Yes you do. I can tell."

"Mom I'm trying to enjoy my meal here. If you keep talking like that I'm going to my room." she threatened.

"Ok then I won't." The room was silent for a moment. Only the sound of them eating could be heard. Occasionally, her mother would look up at her.

"So how was soccer?" she smiled, breaking the silence.

"Mom!"

"What?" she giggled.

Frustrated, she pushed her plate away. "I'm going to my room."

"What did I say? I only asked about soccer." she laughed.

"No, you're asking me about Tom." she responded, getting up from the table.

"Come on admit it. You like Tom." she laughed.

"I'm going to bed." she said, walking away. She marched to her bedroom and slammed the door. Frustrated, she took a shower and got ready for bed. She pulled the covers back and fluffed her pillow. She brushed her damp hair back with her hand and laid down. She closed her eyes with the thoughts of Tom on her mind.

She woke up to the sound of the alarm. Squinting, she look over at the clock to turn it off. Realizing the time, she quickly jumped out of bed. In a matter of minutes, she was dressed and ready to go. "Good morning mom. I'll see you later." she rushed, grabbing an apple on the way out.

"Sweetie you need to eat!"

"Don't have time. Gotta prepare for the game. Is Tom here yet?" she asked, biting into a peach.

"He's out in the front yard."

"We'll be out front practicing. Mom, please don't disturb us. We have a big game tonight." she rushed, closing the door behind her.

"Hi Tom. Are you ready for practice?" she greeted him.

"Ready as I'll ever be." he smiled.

"Ok. Lets take our places. You stand over there and I'll stand here. I'm going to give you the ball first." she continued. She tossed him the ball.

Instead of catching it, he butted back to her.

"I'm impressed." she smiled, kicking it back to him.

"Great teacher." he smiled, tossing it between his feet as he ran past her.

She stood there for a moment smiling.

He finally kicked the ball back to her. She manipulated the ball for a moment then passed it back to him. They carried on for three hours.

"Ok, I think you're ready." she breath, trying to catch her breath. "Go home and get you some rest before the game. You'll need it.

"Ok." he breath, trying to catch his breath. "I'll see you soon." he breathed walking away.

"Oh, I almost forgot. Wait here." she breath, running into the house.

"Here's my uniform." she smiled, handing over all her soccer equipment. "This cap here is a gift though. I made it a week ago."

"Thanks." he smiled. His heart skipped a beat. He was pleased to have it. It made him feel close to her.

"The game starts at eight this evening so be on the North side at the park at 7 p.m. and don't be late. And bring your girlfriend." she smiled.

"O . . . K, he answered, confused.

Waving, he walked away.

"Sweetie, it's time for supper." he mom whispered, peeping her head through the screen door.

She walked in and closed the door behind her.

"Mom, I'm going to clean myself up and I'll be down." she said, going up the stairs.

"Alright." she answered, placing a plate on the table.

Forty minutes later, she came down to join her mother.

"I'm so excited about this game. I can't wait to see how Tom does." she carried on.

"We have worked so hard and . . ." she continued.

Her mother nodded her head. She couldn't get a word in. She just smiled as her daughter talked about Tom and the game.

"Mom you are coming to the game, right?" she continued.

Her mother said nothing. She was in a daze.

"Mom." she said, tapping her hand.

"Hugh?

"You are coming to the game aren't you?"

"Oh yes Sweetie. I wouldn't miss it for the world."

"Ok. Well I'm going up stairs to get some rest before the game." she said, kissing he mother on the cheek.

"Alright."

"Wake me up if the alarm doesn't"

"Ok Sweetie."

"Thanks mom."

"Love you too."

Setting her alarm, she went to sleep. Hours later, the alarm went off. She felt like she had just laid down.

"Sweetheart it's time to get up." her mother said, peeping her head in her room.

"Thanks mom." she yawned, getting up. She changed her clothes and washed her face. After cleaning her room, she ran down stairs.

"Ok mom. I'll see at the game. Be sure to get there at eight. The game starts at eight. Don't forget.

"Ok Sweetie." she yelled from the front living room.

"I'll see you later. Love you."

"Love you too!" she hollard back. It was 7 p.m. sharp when she arrived at the park.

In search of Tom, she spotted a bench and took a seat.

She positioned herself and stretched her leg across the bench to make sure no one could bump it. In search for him, she examined the fields. Finally, she spotted the team. They were standing around in their shin guards and tube socks drinking water and Gatorade. The black and white cougar on their jerseys lived up to it's name. After winning six games they were on a winning streak. She looked over and saw Tom. He was standing around talking to his friends. She searched for his girlfriend but there was no girl in sight, only the players.

"Hey Tom!" she shouted, waving to get his attention.

He looked up at her and waved, smiling. Sighing with anticipation, she folded her arms. He was a working progress. There he stood wearing her number. The number seven that she had maintained for so many years. She hoped his skills could live up to her expectations. Besides, she had a reputation to uphold. He rotated his head and shoulders to loosen up. He appeared to be ready but deep inside he was a nervous wreck. After all this would be his first game.

"I'm over here mom!" she yelled, waving her mother down.

"Have they started yet?" she asked, taking a seat beside her.

"No not yet."

"Where is Tom?" she smiled.

"Right over there." she answered, pointing in his direction.

"He looks really handsome in that outfit." she smiled, looking at Corina.

"Mom. Don't start. I'm trying to watch the game here."

She looked over at the referee and his two assistances. Winning the game was irrelevant to them. Their main concern was the safety of the players. The referee blew his whistle to get the players attention. The players slowly moved to the middle of the field. Pointing and signaling, the referee explained the rules of the game. He flipped a coin to initiate the game. Both teams positioned themselves on their side of the field. Each player stood ten yards away from the ball. The first kick off was in their opponent's favor, the Tigers. During the first thirty minutes of the game they had control of the ball. The Cougars were down by two points. Biting her nails, Corina wondered if the Cougars would win or lose. She knew how hard Tom had practiced. Once the ball was in the Cougars control, one teammate kicked the ball over the field line. The Tigers had control of the ball once more. Tom's opponent shuffled the ball in his direction. He saw an opportunity and cocked his leg between hers. Taking control of the ball, he drove the ball back to his team.

The ball suddenly approached Tom with full force. Tom eagerly took control of the ball. He spotted an opening and took it. He was so in tuned with winning that he forgot his teammate was a woman. He kicked it straight to her. Dodging her opponent, she passed the ball to her teammate. From player to player the ball was passed.

Giving each player a small moment of pleasure, they kept the ball in sequence. It finally reached Tom again.

"Go T.C!" his supporters cheered as he rotated the ball down the field. They watched Tom effortlessly keep the ball in motion. It looked as if he had been playing for years. Keeping the ball in control, he moved closer to the field goal.

"Keep it going! You're almost there!" Corina shouted. By then she was standing up. Obviously, she had forgotten about her injury. Making his final kick, Tom jumped in mid air and kicked the ball. The ball traveled full speed ahead, slamming into the field goal. The weight of his body dropped to the ground as he made the winning score. The crowd roared with victory. His team members rushed towards him and assisted him to his feet. Cheering him on with pats on the back, they group hugged him. Corina somehow limped past them and hugged Tom. Her arms were tightly wrapped around his neck. His arms around her tiny waist. So overwhelmed with winning, it lasted a few minutes. Invading his personal space, her cheek touched his. Their gaze was suddenly locked. Unsure of what to say, he moved in closer at kissing length. She realized her personal space had been violated and quickly pulled away. "Congratulations." she nervously smiled as she slowly backed away. "Where's your girlfriend?" she asked.

"She's here." he smiled.

"Where?" she asked, reluctantly in search of her.

"Standing in front of me." he smiled.

"Oh." she shyly smiled. Pushing her hair behind her ear, she looked down at the ground.

Butterflies danced in her belly to the good news. Slowly, she walked back to her seat. She could still feel his glance.

"I'll see you tomorrow." he called from behind.

She turned to take one final look at him. "OK." she smiled then turned away. She was right. He was still watching her. He could no longer hear the cheering that surrounded him. Only the sound of her footsteps as she walked away to join her mother. He stood there watching her til she disappeared. The players hung out a little longer to celebrate. As the evening got closer they slowly went their separate ways. Tom spotted a can from a distance. In deep thought, he kicked it around to practice his soccer moves. He wondered what would become of he and Corina.

"That was a good game back there." Officer Dolopis said.

"The best." Larke added.

"Tom did you hear us?" Officer Dolopis asked.

"Hugh? Oh yeah. Thanks."

"Where is your mind at?" Larke asked. "Oh, I forgot. He must be thinking of Corina."

Officer Dolopis laughed.

"Why don't you just move in with them?" he teased.

"Hey you guys go ahead without me. I left something back at the park.

"Who? Corina?" Larke teased.

Without responding, he turned back. His mind was too tied up on the cap that Corina had given him. He finally reached the empty field. "Great! There it is." he breathed, picking it up. He dusted it off and placed it on his head. That cap was dear to him because Corina had given it to him as a gift.

His thoughts of her prolonged his trip back home. He finally reached home. The sound of crickets told that everyone was in bed. He slowly went into the house and tiptoed up to his room. Getting ready for bed, he eased underneath the blanket and went to sleep.

The next morning the tour guide decided to take the guys site seeing. Officer Dolopis and Larke came down.

"Where is Tom.?" he asked.

Snickering, Officer Dolopis and Larke looked at each other.

"I'm guessing Corina's." Officer Dolopis answered.

"Ok. Let's go." he sighed.

"Well Larke, I guess that leaves you and me now." Officer Dolopis smiled.

"I guess so."

"Where are we off to today?" Larke asked.

"I thought maybe we could go for a swim." he answered.

"Yippi! I love swimming." the child cheered.

"Great! I'll grab my swim shorts." Officer Dolopis said.

"Me too." Larke added.

"Ok, ready." Officer Dolopis answered, coming down the stairs.

"Alright let's go."

Leaving, Larke pulled the door behind him. The tour guide led the way.

Traveling eastward, he took them to the deep oceans. Officer Dolopis could feel the warm sand gushing between his toes. He noticed some surf boards sitting near a snack stand. There was a sign posted slightly above the snack stand. "Take one but return it when finished."

I guess that means we don't have to pay for a surf board." He smiled, grabbing one. He could see huge waves dancing above the waters.

"Officer Dolopis wait up." Larke called out. The deep sands slowed his progress as he attempted to catch up with Officer Dolopis.

Finally reaching the waters, Officer Dolopis laid across his board. He could feel the cold waters roll underneath his belly as he pushed his way into the water. After getting so far out, he stood up. He could see a huge wave approaching. Guiding his board to keep his balance, he swayed. Huge waves sheltered him. He could feel the waters pushing him as the wave towered over him. Still keeping his balance, he swayed. Then came another wave. This one was much too big. It overtook him. He collapsed underneath the waters. He felt something brush against this leg. He dipped underneath to take a look. It was a dolphin. He swam back to the surface. The dolphin circled around him. It got a little closer. It nudged him in the side then started making noise. Suddenly, the dolphin stood up on the tip of his tail and started dancing on top of the water. Officer Dopolis finally realized that he wanted to play. He grabbed hold of it's dorsal fin. Suddenly, he pulled him down underneath the waters. He was swimming full speed. Bubbles came out of Officer Dolopis' mouth as he looked around. He saw sea creatures that he had never seen before. He peddled further underneath to get a better view. He could see all types of sea creatures and plants. He was amazed with the things he saw. He saw pink and yellow seahorses. There were splashes of colors that filled the bottom. He swam his way back to the top. From a distance, he could see a great whale. Water was spurting from the top of its head. It looked as if there was something sitting on top of the water spurt coming from its blowhole. Officer Dolopis moved closer. He could see a man from far off. The man waved at him. Confused, he waved back. He swam back to land.

"Man you're not going to believe what I just saw." he told Larke.

"What happened?"

"I went under water. I saw the most awesome creatures down there."

And there was this man sitting on top of a water spurt coming from a whales' blowhole." he continued.

"Sounds amazing. All I saw were fish. I can't swim that deep."

"Sorry." he sympathized.

Mr. Dolopis, Can I bury you in the sand? Pl...ea.......se?" she begged, pulling him by the arm.

"Sure Sweetheart." he smiled, following her.

"You know you could really learn to swim if you put your mind to it." the tour guide continued.

"But what if I drown?" he said, finding a spot on the beach towel.

"You won't." he encouraged.

"If you say so. Maybe I'll give it a try next time." he answered, looking down as the girl dumped sand on top of Officer Dolopis then abandoning him.

"I'm going to get you for this." You wait til I get free!" Officer Dolopis, threatened.

Giggling, she ran off and started building a sand castle.

Larke suddenly began laughing. He could only see his head. By then, the tour guide was laughing.

"Guys, don't just sit there. Help me out of this." he pleaded.

After a couple of more laughs, they felt pity for him and dug him out.

"Where is that little munchkin?" he asked, finally free. He spotted her behind a huge umbrella. She screamed and ran. "I'm going to get you!" he grinned, chasing her. He finally caught up to her. He lifted her and swung her around. She laughed, nonstop. He wrestled her to ground and tickled her til she was blue in the face.

"Hey look ice cream." Larke pointed, interrupting their playtime.

Officer Dolopis and the child stopped and looked. There was a man sitting alone on a bench. He was mixing crushed ice and milk. They slowly walked towards him. They watched him pour the mixture into a churning machine.

Wow! How did he do that?" the girl asked, watching it go in a liquid form and come out creamy on the other end.

"Would you all like to try one?" the man finally asked.

"Sure." they smiled, nodding their heads yes.

Delighted, he handed them a cone.

"Mmmm, this is great! Aren't you going to try one Mr. Dolopis?" the girl asked.

"Naw, I'm lactose intolerant." he answered, reluctantly.

"What's latose intolerbant?" she continued.

"It means that my body will not allow me to eat ice cream or I could get sick."

"That's terrible. Everybody likes ice cream." she said, concerned.

"You'll be fine. Try one." the man insisted.

"Alright" he agreed, still unsure.

He passed him an ice cream cone.

Carefully, Officer Dolopis sampled it. He could feel the cool sensation against his tongue. It was smooth. The sweetness left a lasting taste on his tongue.

"Mmm, this is good." he smile.

"I told you it was good." the girl smiled, licking her lips.

Taking another lick, he wrapped his tongue around the scoop. Surprisingly, it didn't bother him.

"Hey where did the tour guide go?" Larke asked, still licking his cone.

"There he is." he answered, tilting his head in his direction. The tour guide was standing underneath a huge tent. There were tables and buckets toppled over with rolls and pastries.

"Bracelets! My favorite." the girl smiled, walking away.

"Would you like to try it on?" the nice lady asked.

"Yes." she smiled, taking a seat.

The lady placed the bracelet around the girl's wrist.

"It's beautiful. You made this yourself?"

"Yes." the lady smiled.

Officer Dolopis walked away, leaving them alone to their girl talk. He approached the tour guide at the next table.

"Hello how are you?" the tour guide smile.

"I'm fine."

"Can I get three guacamoles . . . two cantaloupes and . . ." he requested, pointing to a table decorated with lots of fruit and vegetables. Officer Dolopis noticed a young man approaching the tour guide from behind. Suspicious, Officer Dolopis watched his every move. He looked over at the girl to make sure she was not in harm's way. She was still talking to the lady.

"I have one almost like it but I didn't wear it today. I never leave home without it. It's just that we went swimming and I didn't want to lose it so I took it off." the child babbled on.

Officer Dolopis looked over at the man again. He watched him as he looked over the items to make his selection. Selecting an orange, he walked away.

Suddenly, Officer Dolopis tossed his cone and rushed towards the fruit stand.

Still, the lady across from them, didn't notice anything. She was still talking to the child.

"That's too bad. I wanted to see it."

I'm sure it's just as beautiful. What color is it?" the lady asked.

"It's pink and white. My m."

"Stop thief!" Officer Dolopis ordered, interrupting them. Suddenly, Officer Dolopis took a dive at the man. The child began screaming. She watched them as they fell upon a table, breaking it in half. Rolls and cakes went up in the air. Fruits and baskets were scattered on the ground. The man managed to get up and attempted to flee. Officer Dolopis pulled his feet from underneath then wrestled him down. Fruit and baskets were everywhere. Finally gaining his balance, Officer Dolopis grabbed him by the collar. "Did you know it is against the law to steal?" he accused, pulling him to his feet. The crowd surrounded them. Some of them turned their faces away. They were displeased at this type of behavior.

"Stop! He's not stealing." the tour guide intervened.

"Then what is he doing!" he breathed, binding the man's arms behind him.

"Mr. Dolopis, everything is free here!" the tour guide sighed. He shook his head in disappointment.

"What do you mean?" Officer Dolopis asked, turning him a loose. Dusting himself off, the young man stared at him. He was petrified.

"Mr. Dolopis, all the food that is grown here belongs to everyone." the tour guide explained. The girl was holding his hand and rubbing her tearful eyes.

Officer Dolopis' face grew hot. Exhaling, he walked up to the man.

"I'm so sorry!" he pleaded.

Appalled, the man said nothing. He checked himself for injuries then walked away, shaking his head in disbelief.

Officer Dolopis dropped his head to hide his embarrassment. His face was burning with shame.

"Man what is wrong with you?" Larke asked, painfully laughing.

"Shut up!" He whispered, gritting his teeth. Officer Dolopis was quiet for the rest of the day. For the first time he actually missed home.

"Hey check that out." Larke whispered, nudging Officer Dolopis to get his attention.

He looked up. He could see two twins sitting on a buggy. They were pushing and shoving each other. They appeared to be quarrelling. Their voices got louder as they approached.

"I am the eldest so I should be the one to drive the buggy. It's my birth right." one of them argued.

"No you're not. I am." the other answered, pushing.

"I'll give you this cup of soup if you let me. I know you're hungry." he bribed.

"Alright." his brother smiled, passing him the harness strap.

"Awe! Giddy up!" he ordered, pulling at the horse. Suddenly, the buggy took off, leaving dust behind.

Officer Dolopis and Larke looked at each other and began laughing.

"Where did the tour guide go?" Larke grinned, finally getting control of himself.

"He was just standing here a minute ago."

"Hey, lets go to the south side. I hear there's a jungle over there. I want to see the animals." Larke suggested.

"I don't know about that. I think we should wait for the tour guide to return. I can't handle anymore excitement." Officer Dolopis answered, skeptical.

"Come on. He won't even notice us missing." he pressed.

"Well . . . alright. Just as long as we come right back."

Although he was going along with him, Officer Dolopis was still uneasy.

From a distance, they could hear a loud motor. They followed the noise. They noticed a man driving a tractor. He was grazing a huge corn field.

Suddenly, the ground began trembling. They were not that far from the jungle. The sound of trumpeting elephants crossed their path. One elephant approached them from behind but detoured to keep from running into them. They looked over to the left only to see another one approaching. They ran behind some trees to escape. They came upon a quiet remote lake. Giant lily pads that strayed from a nearby citrus fruit garden covered this lake. They watched a crocodile slowly approach the clear waters. Inch by inch it slowly disappeared underneath. Occasionally, the sound of flapping wings could be heard from behind the trees. Officer Dolopis fixated his attention on a turtle nearby. It was slowly chewing on a berry. Officer Dolopis noticed a pile of berries sitting near a rock. He smiled.

Suddenly, from nowhere a stork leaped down and grabbed a mouth full of fish. He watched it as it spread it's beautiful wings and take off.

"Hey look!" Larke whispered, holding him back. From a distance, a man was standing near the waters painting. Larke smiled for a moment. He remembered how much his father enjoyed painting.

"Hey Mister!" he finally whispered. Slowly, he approached from behind. Although his back was turned to him, he could feel a connection.

"Excuse me Sir!" he continued, gently touching him on the shoulder.

"Yes? Can I help you?" the man answered, slowly turning around.

Larke looked at him then at his painting. Recognizing the painting, he suddenly began panting. His heart began pumping full speed. His eyes bucked with fear. He was speechless. He had seen this picture before. It was a painting of he and his mother. His mother had the exact same picture back at home.

"How can I help you young man?" he asked, looking at him then at Officer Dolopis.

Taking a deep swallow, Larke finally uttered, "Papa? Is that you?"

"You know this man?" Officer Dolopis asked, puzzled.

"Yes, he's my father." he tearfully answered.

"Larke!" he answered, starting to recognize him.

""It's been so long. We've missed you so much." he cried, embracing him.

"How's your mother?" he cried.

"She's well. She had to get a job after you left."

"I never wanted to leave you and your mother." He admitted.

"I know Pop. Oh this here is my buddy Officer Dolopis." he smiled.

"It's nice to meet you."

"My pleasure." He answered.

"Your Aunt Ellen is here and so is your grandparents. Come on I want them to see how much you've changed." He continued, putting his arm around him.

Walking, Larke turned and asked, "aren't you coming Officer Dolopis?"

"No you go ahead. Spend some time with your family. I'm going to head back. The tour guide might be looking for me." he answered, fighting his tears back.

"Alright. It was nice knowing you. Thanks for everything." Larke smiled.

"It was my pleasure." he answered. He watched them walk away arm and arm. He finally began heading back towards the village.

He looked up at the sky. It was getting late. When he reached home, he noticed the tour guide having supper alone.

"Where is Larke?" he asked.

"He ran into his dad."

"That's great." he smiled

"Will I ever get a chance to see any of my loved ones?"

"No." he answered, getting up to clear the table. He began placing the dishes into the sink.

"Why not?" Officer Dolopis asked, irritated.

"Because you are going back home tomorrow."

He stood there for a moment watching him clean a plate.

"What do you mean?" he asked, getting upset.

"You're on vacation, remember? You have to go back."

"Why? There's nothing back there for me. I like it here." he complained.

"You have unfinished business."

"What kind of business?" he continued.

"You'll understand when you get there. Why don't you go upstairs and get some rest. Your boat leaves at 9 a.m. sharp."

Reluctantly, Officer Dolopis dragged himself upstairs. He took a shower then climbed into bed. He tossed and turned all night. He fixated on the moon just outside his window and finally drifted off to sleep.

The next morning the sun beamed into his face. Not wanting to get up, he stretched his arms and legs. He finally got up and began packing his things.

"Alright I think that's it." he said, coming down the stairs. He stood there for a moment with bundles of his belongings underneath his armpits. He was prepared to return home.

The tour guide and the little girl were sitting at the table having breakfast.

"Don't you want to eat before you leave?" he asked, arranging a spot for him to sit.

"I'm not hungry." he sharply answered.

"Alright it's your call. Come on lets go." he said, grabbing his hat.

"Wait for me!" the little girl yelled, putting her sweater on. The tour guide led the way to the dock. The little girl grabbed hold of Officer Dolopis' hand as he slowly followed behind him. Officer Dolopis felt strange that morning. He felt divided. Part of him wanted to stay but another half was anxious to return home. He wondered what he was going to say to his friends and family. How would he explain where he had been all this time? Finally reaching his destination, he lifted the little girl. She kissed him on the cheek and whispered, "tell mommy and daddy I'll be waiting for them."

He put her back down. "Bye Sweetie." he smiled, puzzled at what she had said. He could hear the loud engine. Attempting to climb onto the boat, he yelled, "You never told me your name!"

"It's Moses." the tour guide answered.

Appalled at his response, he gazed back at him. Missing his step, he fell into the water. The water was extremely cold. He could feel his body being lifted as rescuers pulled him out of the water. He was in and out of consciousness. He couldn't make out what had just happened. All he could hear was the sound of the engine and voices. Still half awake, he could see the little girl. He could see her from a slight distance. "Bye Mr. Dolopis!" she smiled, waving good bye. He noticed a bracelet on her wrist. He attempted to lift his head but couldn't. His eyelids became heavy. He could feel the boat moving. Wanting to turn back, he cried, "wait. wait a minute. Keva don't go." He fixated his view on her. Tiny voices began fading. Like a tiny image in the center of a beaming bulb, they slowly disappeared. His eyes got heavier. Soon the bright light got smaller and smaller. Then it was gone. He had fallen asleep. Hours had passed. His journey had been long. Coughing, he opened his teary eyes. After six months in a coma, he had awaken only to realize that it was all a mere dream.

"Hi Sweetie. It's good to see you." his wife cried. She smothered him with her hugs and kisses.

"Do you happen to have a bible? he managed to ask.

"Yeah sure, I have one in my purse." she answered, puzzled. Reaching for it, she asked, "Is there something wrong?" looking back at the family. She handed it over to him. Looking in the back of the index, he looked up redemption then turned to the scripture. He read it. Ecstatic over what he had just read, he cried with joy.

"Honey what is it?" she asked. Holding her in his arms, he said nothing. Once he was released from the hospital, he went to visit Monica. Nervously gripping the flowers, he rang the doorbell.

"Yes?" she smiled. Her husband came up from behind.

"Hi Mr. and Mrs. Murlette. I'm sorry to be dropping by unannounced. I'm Officer Dolopis. I just wanted to inform you that your daughter is alright. She awaits you on the day of your resurrection." he smiled, crying.

"Thank you for those kind words." Mrs. Murlette smiled, hugging him.

"These are for you." he smiled, giving her the flowers.

"Would you like to come in?" she asked.

"Sure, don't mind if I do." he smiled, walking in. He gently closed the door behind him.